NAKYTA'S

GLITTER

Volume II

Nicole On the Run

SIMPLY NICOLE

DEDICATION

I would like to dedicate this book to everyone that said I would
not amount to anything. To everyone that counted me out,
judged and made me feel less than for being different. Hopefully,
your souls find eternal peace. The potter wants to use you again.
There is an artist waiting to be discovered in all of us. Keep
chiseling until that masterpiece is discovered.

~Ase~

ACKNOWLEDGMENTS

First and foremost, I would like to give thanks to The Creator. I finally understand my purpose. Thank you for seeing me fit for this assignment.

To my mother and father,

thank you for instilling in me that I can do

anything I put my mind to.

In the words of Snoop Dogg,

"I want to thank me

I want to thank me for believing in me

I want to thank me for doing all this hard work.

I want to thank me for having no days off

I want to thank me for never quitting

I want to thank me for always being a giver and trying to give more than I receive.

I want to thank me for trying to do more right than wrong.

I want to thank me, for just being me at all times."

~Uncle Snoop~

I especially want to thank my loyal fan base that is incarcerated in DC, Maryland, Virginia and Atlanta. I do it for you all. God's got you. Believe that. I love you all.

All praises due to the most high.

Chapter 1

Introduction

What happened to my life? In a matter months, I went from; Nicole Edwards, the young single mother to a young toddler daughter and a nurse, with a promising career ahead of me; to Nicole Williams, a young insecure wife to a husband that cheated on me and got me pregnant in an effort to save our relationship. No one knew that Montez and I, had secretly married on April 01, 2018 in Las Vegas. He wanted to show me that he had good intentions and wanted the best for my daughter and I. According to him, he did not care if he had to spend a lifetime proving that his heart belonged to me, it would be a life well spent because I was worth it. Montez knew all the right shit to say to make me melt. One glance into his eyes was enough to make me do whatever he wanted me to do. When I looked into his eyes, I saw God and that made it easy for me to willingly submit to him. Within a few months of marriage, I had turned into a person that I would wrestle with recognizing for the rest of my life. In my head, my job was to protect my family as best as I could. You know? By Any Means Necessary! This was the first time that my daughter had a chance to have a real father and call someone daddy. He was good to her! The way he admired and cared for Jenesis was unbelievable. You would think that she was his daughter.

In a few short months, they had become inseparable and I swore they had started to resemble each other. Every now and again, I like to reminisce back on when my life was simple. I was innocent and doing the best that I could for myself and my family. Things took a turn for the worse and now I am living my life on the run, to avoid prosecution. The ones that are suffering the most are my children. They do not even know me anymore, especially the twins. All I find myself thinking about is the hurt I feel for abandoning my children and leaving the burden of raising them on Aunt Lu. I no longer had my nursing job and I didn't have my husband either. He was incarcerated, hopefully feeling all the hurt and pain that he caused his family. There was nothing left for me to do but shake up the judge and prosecutors. I had to scare them into throwing out the case against Montez and I. Even though Montez deserved to be incarcerated, I still love him and want us to be a family again. I daydream about the kind of father he would be to Angel and Messiah. That is what is keeping me from hating him.

Within four months of being on the run, I had come across so many problems. First Aunt Lu called me to inform me that Montez was thinking about turning states evidence. He had been transferred to an out of state facility. As luck would have it, he was moved to the same facility as my dad, a.k.a. "THE BEAR". She also informed me that her health had been declining and that she was uncertain of how much longer she could remain the children's custodial guardian. Her phone call was concerning. Some things she did not want to tell me over the phone. Lu said she needed to be faced to face before she could come clean about some shit that would eventually come out in court. After ending the call with LuAnn, I expressed my concern to Jesse as he drove. My exact words were, "Bruh, if that bitch betrayed me too, I would kill her! On God, Moe imma kill her". I've taken so many losses and there is no way I could bounce back from any betrayal from my closest relative. Jesse tried his hardest to persuade me that I was overthinking the matter. I believed him until I put in a call to one of the dirty detectives scheduled to testify against Montez. It is amazing how people will compromise their dignity and morals for money. All it took was money to make some shit go away.

Detective Rodriguez informed me that a close family member of mine had turned states' evidence and that it was a good idea if I just disappeared forever. How can I just disappear forever? I have three kids that depend on me. It had been made clear that if I returned, no mercy would be spared on me. I would be brought in for several murders. The amount of money and connections I had would prove to be pointless. My job is to contain my anger and impulsiveness. I know Aunt Lu is a rat now. The only thing that is boggling my mind is why? We have thirty years of secrets between the two of us. Why now? After all this! The next of kin for the twins would be Montez's mother and that bitch is one marble away from being declared insane. Ain't no way in two hells I would let that bitch get my children.

Chapter 2

Jesse's Dilemma

We finally came to a truck stop in Vermont. Jesse got out to stretch. He had drove ten straight hours and had cramps in his legs. After stretching, he helped me off the rig. He noticed that my skin was cool and clammy. There was blood on my shirt and on the seat. I didn't think anything of it because I had just given birth days ago, but Jesse was worried. "Do you want to go get checked out", he asked nervously. I ignored him and made my way to the woman's bathroom. We both went separate ways to shower and met back up inside the food court. I grabbed feminine hygiene products and a first aid kit, while Jesse reached for 2 burner phones and a bottle of water. He gave me some money and asked that I get him 2 franks with sauerkraut so that he could make a private call outside. I agreed and told him not to expect any change back. Jesse laughed as he walked through the door looking back at me picking up last-minute items. He turned the corner and stood on the side of the store so that he could see whenever I walked out of the door.

Jesse called his wife. Roxy was infuriated with him and would not accept any excuse he would come up with. He had been on the road for over 4 months this time. Normally he would go home for the weekend at least twice a month. As my needs grew greater, he began catering to that need and in the process abandoned his wife and son, Rodney. Jesse and Roxy had been married for 4 years. He expressed his love for his wife to me in the middle of random conversations that we had had while driving. Just as much as he expressed his love for his family, he expressed his concerns and frustrations. Jesse did not feel loved, he felt needed. The only time his wife cared to be affectionate with his was when he brought his paycheck home. The relationship with his fourteen-year-old son was estranged because of the career path he took. Rodney had gotten used to seeing his dad every day and for the past two years it has been limited to some weekends per month. Roxy yelled into the receiver at Jesse. She was miserable at this point. None of her needs were being met. He started paying the bills himself and had stop sending leisure money to Roxy. Jesse pointed out that the last time she called to say, "I love you, be safe, or thank you", had been well over a year ago.

According to Roxy, she had taken enough of Jesse's shit and wanted a divorce. She claimed that she could prove infidelity and that Jesse abandoned the family. "Do you think that I am dumb, I know that you are sleeping with that bitch. You walk out on us to go play hero to a bitch that can't hold her own shit together. What are you? Captain Save-A-Hoe now"? "Roxy you are wrong", Jesse calmly replied. "I want a divorce", Roxy yelled at him. Jesse turned his back towards the stores entrance and held his head down. He made every attempt to explain that he had not slept with anyone and that it was just business. Roxy continued to yell at him and call him degrading names. Jesse was so deep in the conversation with his wife that he didn't notice when I walked out of the store and stood directly behind him. He grew more frustrated at Roxy's insinuations that he said to her, "Bitch, do you want to know why I stopped coming home? You do not want me, you need me. You sit at home all day watching reality TV shows. You don't cook and you barely clean. You want me to do it all and all you do is nag. When is the last time you called without wanting or needing something? If I were sleeping with anyone other than you, what would it matter? I have to pay you for that pussy, which by the way, tastes like despair and it's not hitting on shit.

What man in their right mind would put up with a tacky hoe such as yourself? You do not bring anything to the table. Nothing but problems and kids from another nigga. Bitch you are lucky that I have been faithful thus far. You want a divorce? Fine with me. Back to the ghetto you go. I doubt that you ever loved me. We just got a kid together bitch! There may be some truth in your accusations, Roxy. Here is where you're wrong though. I don't like Nicole; I am in love with her. Do you remember that innocent teenage love? That's what makes me happy". Jesse slammed the phone down to the ground, smashing it into pieces before he turned around to see me standing in shock with my mouth wide open.

We stood there, staring at each other in silence for at least a minute. Jesse broke the silence and said, "Shit Cole, you weren't supposed to hear that. It was not supposed to come out that way. I never wanted you to learn the truth like this". I was still in shock and turned away in disbelief to walk back to the truck. The ride to Canada was awkward. You could hear a pin drop. Jesse wanted to address what happened, but I would not break my silence. I forced myself to sleep as Jesse drove, only waking up to go to the restroom. He grew tired of my silence after six hours and said, "Fuck this", as he slammed on the brakes. He got out of the truck, slamming the door and throwing his hat to the ground. Jesse walked over to the passenger side of the truck where I was and kicked the tire out of frustration. He opened the door and spun me around by my waist so that I was facing him. Jesse looked deeply into my eyes and demanded that I did the same. He had some shit to get off his chest and needed my undivided attention. He asked for me to be open to receive what he had to say because it was coming from an honest and genuine place.

"I never set out to fall for you Nicole. Al reached out to me with a business proposal. Even though you were amid turmoil, you still carried yourself gracefully. You smiled at me even when I knew you were dying inside. You had no idea of the amount of stress and pressure I was under and yet you still managed to make me laugh. The fact that I am married is what made me keep it strictly business. My marriage ain't shit as you can see, but I still chose to respect you. How long have you been on the road with me? As you know, men have needs. Have you ever seen me pick up another woman or entertain one for that matter? My eyes have been on you and only you for the past four months. You make me feel alive Nicole. These roads get lonely. Look at all the conversations we have had thus far. Imagine not having anyone to talk to. That is my life. I watch you sleep and fall that much more in love with you. I know you don't want to spend your life in a truck with me, but you look safe and at peace when you are asleep, and I feel like I am doing something right. For a moment, it looks like you want to be here. It makes me want to guard your life with my very own. I didn't ask for these feelings. I did not even plan on revealing this to you. It just kind of came out. I am apologetic that you found out the way that you did but I will not apologize for the way I feel about you. I just want to grow closer and I hope that it doesn't make you uncomfortable".

I decided to break my silence by saying, "Jesse, I don't know what to say. This has caught me off guard. I am not uncomfortable; I am just at a loss for words. Give me some more time to process what you are telling me. I respect your honesty and I know that you did not set out to try to win me over. We have spent an immense amount of time together and at the end of the day, we are only human. The universe has a way of rearranging our lives for better or for worse. You must respect the fact that I choose to say nothing until I take it all in. I don't want to speak prematurely. I am not saying you are right or wrong. I could have tried my hand with hitch hiking if it were that serious, but I am still here with you. Just leave me to my thoughts. A lot has taken place in just one day. It'll all be okay".

My words comforted Jesse and he blushed as he walked to the driver's side of the truck. I am slightly relieved and have a better understanding of Jesse's feelings, but still uncomfortable after hearing him out. Jesse knew that he had to file for and get a divorce before he could even entertain the thoughts of a relationship with me. Hell, I am still married my damned self and I am not that kind of lady. No shade to those that are. I grew up believing that there was a special place in hell for people that slept around with married people no matter the circumstance. My dad cheated on my mom and they were married. I watched her heart break a million times before she snapped. I didn't want that to be my fate, so I played by the rules. To my knowledge, Jesse would have to file in the same state that he and Roxy was married in which was New York. It was about three hundred and forty miles from where we were. That was an easy drive to Jesse. He could buss that move in his sleep. I have seen him do it. Jesse put on Erykah Badu and I swear he eagerly made his way out of Vermont and into New York.

Within one hour on the road, Jesse wanted to talk again. He asked questions like, what color gold I preferred between white, rose and yellow. He wanted to know if I preferred a private wedding or a traditional one. I am sure he is eager to move forward but damn; he is really jumping the gun ain't he? It took all the respect in me to reply to his questions in a polite and respectful manner. Regardless of how respectful I was, Jesse still sensed my agitation, which caused him to shut down. I'm not sure if he understands that it is entirely too early to be trying to start a relationship with me. I understand his position, but he does not understand mines. As time went by, the surer I was that I was not interested in Jesse. He was cool as shit, don't get me wrong. It's just that by being on the road, thinking about all the shit that had happened and the pain Montez caused me, it left me salty towards men. Hours of driving had passed, and I would stare out the window, catching glimpses of women. I fantasized about being in a relationship with another woman. As we entered Brooklyn, New York; Jesse asked me if this drive was pointless. He said he got the feeling that I did not feel for him what he felt for me. That was the start of an unnecessary argument. He was adamant that I should have been real back when we were at the last truck stop. "We could have avoided driving to New York. Do you realize that we are only here so that I can file for divorce"?

Listen Jesse, I have been as respectful and considerate of your feelings as I'm gonna be. No one wants to continue to hear this bullshit. You are being well compensated for your troubles. I am in no way responsible for your failed marriage. You are passively treating me like all your problems are my fault. You do not see me crying about my failed marriage. My life will never be the same and my kids will never know the love I have for them. You want sympathy and it is not in me to give. I told you years ago that that bitch was not any good for you, but you did not want to listen. I guess you decided to settle for whatever bitch that batted an eye at your ass since you could not have me at the time. I mean, I get it, I guess. Just shut the fuck up with all your attempts to make me feel bad. It is either you build a bridge and get over it or you let me out this fucking truck right now and go about your business. Surviving is what I do so fuck you!

Before I could say another word, Jesse had back handed the shit out of me. I swear I tasted the blood before it pooled from my lip. My head spun around and when I looked up at him, I noticed that he looked as if he enjoyed hitting me. It was almost like he had waited for that moment his entire life. Ol' skinny bastard! Make no mistake about it, I was turned on and before I could respond, he leaned in to kiss my bloody lip. I gasped out of shock and fear that he would strike me again. His kiss was soft and passionate. I learned a lot in that kiss. This man was madly in love with me. My lady parts started running its natural nectar which prompted me to straddle his lap and kiss him back. As we made out on the drivers' seat of his truck, Jesse pushed me off him and said that he didn't picture our first encounter this way. He told me to put my seat belt on as he drove to the nearest truck stop in New York. While there, he researched all the five-star hotels in the vicinity and decided to give *"The Knickerbocker"* a visit.

The room was absolutely breath taking. I could live here forever! The bathroom had ceiling to floor windows that overlooked *Times Square*. The jacuzzi bathtub could easily seat four people in it. Jesse ran me a hot bubble bath and put on my favorite station on *Spotify*, which is *Donald Glover, a.k.a. Childish Gambino*. That man is a lyrical genius, a true artist. I could listen to his songs on repeat for the rest of my natural life and never get tired of hearing him. As I laid back in the tub and closed my eyes, Jesse came in with a tray of strawberries covered in white chocolate and champagne filled goblets. He asked if he could light some candles to set the mood and I agreed.

I closed my eyes and reminisced back to the time that Jenesis's father took me to the *Capital Arena* in DC to see *Donald Glover a.k.a. Childish Gambino*. Tez knew that he was my favorite artist. Imagine watching your favorite artist on stage performing and abruptly stops and leave the stage. The TV monitors around the arena shows Donald walking the halls. Then he comes back into the arena but this time he's mingling with the audience. A peaceful pandemonium breaks out and before I knew it, Donald is walking down my section and over towards me. I instantly began screaming and crying like the true fan that I was. He stops dead in his tracks and looks over at me and smiled. I swear to God this really happened. He reaches out his hand and awaits my hand and held it for about five seconds. He began to walk away, still smiling and looking at me. I am sure his security team nudged him to remind him that he had a show to put on. Donald was lost in my eyes and smile. The energy that ran through our hands felt amazing. I did not wash my left hand for an entire week. Nor did I allow anyone to touch it. His hand was so soft, his smile was so pure. I orgasmed moments before he let my hand go.

Jesse interrupted my orgasmic daydream to let me know that he was going to the gym downstairs. He totally pissed me off. Like dude, I am dreaming of Gambino, you can go to hell and never come back for all I care. I did not say that out loud, but I damn sure thought it. How dare he interrupt greatness? My garden is pouring nectar and for the first time in ten months, I am in heat. Jesse ain't no D.G, but he will do. I asked that he not go anywhere because I wanted to talk to him. As I made my way out the tub and into the bedroom, Jesse asked me what was up. He stood near the fireplace clutching his glass of *Courvoisier* on the rocks. You can tell when a female is up to something. I made my way over to him and leaned in to smell his neck. The hairs on his neck stood up, which was a clear indication that he was excited or nervous. I hoped for the latter but whichever it was, I didn't care. My nose and lips lightly stroked the back of his neck and he let out a sensual moan as my hands made its way down his pants. A rather hard and large package awaited me. The saying is true ladies; skinny men carry big guns. GOT DAMN! I cannot wait to feel this motherfucker. Shit! Tez was girthy but Jesse is both long and girthy.

He ran his hand between my thighs and felt the moisture. Confused by it all, he slid his index finger inside me and was immediately blown away at how wet I had gotten. He asked me what I had gotten myself into while I was in the tub. Instead of answering him, I pushed him towards the nearest chair so that I could mount him. With *Donald Glover* still playing in the background, I climbed on top of him and grabbed his dick as I slid down on it. We both let out a gasp at the same time. I gasped because after putting his dick in me, I felt full. He gasped because I was extremely wet, and my walls gripped every inch of his dick. It had been ages since Jesse had gotten any pussy. things have moved so fast that neither one of us realized that we were fucking raw. The more I gyrated my hips, the more he tried to push me off him. It was like riding a bull and I was determined not to fall off. He would just have to nut in me! In the moment, the dick felt way too good to stop. *Pop Thieves* came on and I went crazy on the dick, rotating and pouncing to the beat. Jesse pushed me off him one minute into the song. That bull was ready to fire off! He threw me down on the bed and began to feast from my garden. The orgasms came back to back. His lips felt like a blend of mink and velvet.

Oh my God! I had cheated myself from sexual satisfaction for years. I could have had this years ago. Of course, I felt like I played myself. Within 10 minutes, I had climaxed three times. By the time he got up my body was limp. He wasn't done, but I was. Jesse threw my legs around his neck and placed his hands on my breasts. What he did next was unbelievable. He pounded and pounded until I screamed out in pain and pleasure. My legs began to shake uncontrollably as he flipped me over on my stomach. He wanted to fuck in the doggy style position, but my legs were too limp for anything other than laying on my side. That didn't bother him one bit. He went in from the side and gyrated his hips slowly until the next song came on and he could find his rhythm. I happened to look up at him and noticed his face was in shock. He could not quite put his finger on it, but I can tell that he was trying to figure out what was inside my pussy. Before I came out of the bathroom, I had inserted my medium sized rose quartz yoni egg. The benefits are amazing. It is known as the love stone and important to the heart chakra.

Not even two minutes went by and he had pulled out and emptied his load on my right hip. He collapsed on his mess an on me. Panting hard and kissing my neck and face. Neither one of us could talk. We just laid there in a state of euphoria, still in disbelief that we have been intimate after all these years. When I was able to gather my composure, I went in my purse and grabbed my gun. After cocking and pointing it at him, I said, "Bitch, the next time you hit me, you'll be going on a permanent vacation".

He laughed me out like I was a joke. I had to remind him that I had bodies on me already and that he could always add to the collection. The words that he uttered out of his mouth left me flabbergasted. This motherfucker had the gall to tell me that he wanted to go see his son and wanted me to confront his wife based on the conversation I had overheard. Do you know that tingly feeling you get in your soul when you know shit gon' go left? It took over my body and all I could do was shake my head. What could I possibly have to say to Roxy? What does this nigga have up his sleeve? Is he trying to lure me into a trap? No doubt, I can defend myself, but I don't like being blind- sided. NO ONE DOES! It would be a shame for him to want to test me after the lovely evening that we had just had. All kinds of scenarios ran through my head and I just couldn't figure out what he could stand to gain.

Chapter 3

<u>Nicole Meets Roxy</u>

It was a quick drive from Manhattan to the Bronx. I've been to New York a few times, but never the Bronx. The people's accent was thick enough to cut. I had never heard so many Yo's and dead ass B's in my fucking life. Roxy lived on *Sedgwick Avenue* in the most horrible, ran down tower called *River Mill Gardens*. When Jesse parked the truck, I looked at him and asked if he was trying to buy some weed before we went to see Roxy. He laughed and said that this is where she lived. I cringed! Now, I had lived in the ghetto before but never this kind of ghetto. I could smell the gun powder, roach and mice droppings in the air from inside of the truck. There is no way that I can get out! "Aye Jesse, call that bitch and tell her to come outside". He had some serious explaining to do. Why on earth would he have his wife and child living in the gutter. That told me the kind of man he was. Then I thought back to the conversation he had with Roxy while I was in the service station. I had come out in time to hear him tell her that she could go back to ghetto. Maybe she had taken him up on that offer. You know bitches love to prove a point. Looking around, her point must have been that she ain't need him for shit. Now I am curious to see how they are living.

After three sighs, I got out of the truck and followed Jesse towards the tower entrance. There was a booster on every square of the pavement that lead up to the building. Anything you needed was available, from soap to bullets. One guy yelled out, "Yo Ma, you looking mad fly this afternoon; dead ass B, let me take you from that square ass nigga". Jesse ignored the shit! I pulled my gun from the small of my back and walked back to the guy that said something. I smiled at him and grabbed his mouth with my left hand while the right hand held the gun to the side of his nose. In my best New York accent, I said; "Yo daddy, you wanna go on a permanent vacation? Disrespect me like that again and its lights out for you B, dead ass son!" I smooched his face and continued walking as the crowd cheered and laughed his bitch ass out. Jesse laughed too and said that I was crazy. What kind of man allows another man to say some shit like that about him? He heard him just like I heard him. Let me find out Jesse is a lowkey bitch! Nah Moe, on God that shit not gon' fly with me.

After entering the building, Jesse gave me the run down. He told me not to talk to anyone else, not to look at anyone and to never use the elevator. Roxy lived on the third floor, which meant that I had to climb six flights of stairs. It's sounding like a death trap to me and now I am uneasy, which means that I will be quicker to draw my gun. Thank God its fully loaded and waiting on a bitch or a nigga to play with me. I am one hot tempered bitch now and woke up wishing that a motherfucker would. We finally made it to the third floor. I caught an instant contact high after walking through clouds of smoke right before arriving at Roxy's door. Jesse knocked on the door as I stood behind him wondering why he did not have a key. In a split second, all kinds of questions ran through my head. Is this really Roxy's house? Does Jesse live here? Could he be setting me up? Even if that were his plan, I would not hesitate to kill any and everyone. My blood boiled at this point. I want to believe that maybe this is Roxy's mother house or some shit like that. Anything else and its gon' be time to get the party started.

Rodney answered the door, excited to see his dad. Roxy stood behind her son with a look of disappointment and hurt. I was reading her face and picking up on her energy. There was about a thirty second pause of silence as father and son hugged. Here I stand, face to face with the woman that accused me of sleeping with her husband. She would not have a leg to stand on had we not had sex last night. Cuz baby!!!! We got it in last night. Shidddd! My legs are still weak, and I wish this apple head bitch would invite us in so I can sit down. It feels like my insides are going to fall out. I broke the silence by saying, "Hi, my name is Nicole and I presume that you are Roxy? Its' a pleasure to finally meet you". This ugly bitch had the audacity to blurt out that she didn't give a fuck who I was and wanted to know why I was at her door. It took everything in me to say nothing. That caused Jesse and Rodney to look up. All I could think was that this bitch does not know me from a hole in the wall. I will split her shit in front of her rock head ass son and think nothing of it. "Baby girl, you got the game fucked up. You gotta relax Ma! Exactly what is your problem with me? You got it in your head that I have slept with your husband and that is not true. I've been through hell and back and Jesse has been a good friend to me. I would never violate anyone's marriage.

At this point I am sure that playing innocent was the best route to take. Nah, I am not scared of her if that is what you are thinking. The ball is in my court and this bitch will bow down to me. I want to mind fuck her at this point because I did not like her attitude while I introduced myself. She needs to let her guard down enough so that Jesse can do whatever it is that he came to do without her acting like an asshole. I am sure she was expecting me to act rowdy and ghetto, but I know when to hold them and when to fold them. I held my shit together because I know what I am capable of. She does not know my history; and I am sure that if she did, she would be a lot more respectful. She eyeballed me for about ten second before Jesse asked if we could come in. Roxy picked up on something in my eyes and seen that I was not to be fucked with. She agreed to let us in, and I walked past the three of them and made my way to the couch. After sitting down and kicking up my feet, I noticed Roxy looking over at Jesse. I am laughing inside because I bet this bitch is thinking all kinds of shit; meanwhile I am kicked back and do not give a fuck what she is thinking. I would fuck the shit out of her in front of her husband and make her forget why she was even mad. That or shoot her. It didn't matter to me.

Jesse asked Rodney to go into his bedroom so that the adults could talk. Soon after he began explaining to Roxy all his issues with her. Truth be told, I could have stayed in the truck for all this shit. He told Roxy that he did not love her anymore and hadn't in a while. If you could have been a fly on the wall; you would see that she looked over at me as if I were the reason that Jesse did not love her anymore. She had it in her head that I was the reason for his sudden change of heart, and I was not. He talked for what seemed like an hour; while she stood with her hands folded, side eyeing me. Roxy began pacing the floor as Jesse began to talk about me. He stated that he had known me for years and that we initially met back when he did his last bid. "Nicole is like a sister to me Roxy; she was there for me when everyone turned their back on me and now that she's in need of help, I would be wrong to turn my back on her". I had enough of this old ass soap opera scenario, so I interrupted and asked where the bathroom was. Roxy showed me the way and when she turned to walk away, I slapped her on her ass.

Of course, that shocked her and all I could do was smile at her because in my head I was thinking, "damn that thing claps back". I assume that she told Jesse what I had did because when I went back to the living room, he was looking at me funny. Trying not to burst out in laughter, I went into the kitchen and helped myself to the food that had been on the stove cooking. I yelled out into the living room asking if anyone wanted a wine cooler or a shot of *Courvoisier*. This is my girl now! She has all my favorite products in her bathroom and kitchen. Even though I had assumed that she lived in squalor, I still liked her and was reminded to never judge a book by its cover. Roxy finally had the floor to speak and I could sense her confusion. She asked me what the status of my relationship was with my own husband. Can you believe this bitch? Sarcasm took over me and I told her that whatever it was, it ain't no more. "I'm on to better things now baby". I stood up and walked over to her and whispered, "my eyes are on you now," in her left ear. Jesse eyeballs popped out of his head.

Apparently, I made him uncomfortable. I am a female and this dude felt threatened by me. That fed my ego and there is no way I can back down now. I live for a challenge and since I know it disturbs Jesse, I'm all in. He started it. No one told him to downplay the relationship he had with me. At this point, I am insulted and feel like kicking up some shit just because I know I can. I got up and stood behind Roxy; and kissed her neck, while staring into Jesse's eyes. He was livid! He began making excuses for why we had to get back on the road and I shut him down every time. I asked Roxy if it was okay for us to spend the night. After she smirked, she said it would be her pleasure. When I tell you that Jesse was angry, Baby! That nigga was pissed. He asked if he could speak to me in private and I totally ignored him. After looking out the window and realizing that the sun was setting, I asked Jesse to walk me to the truck to get my overnight bag.

He was delighted to oblige because he still wanted to talk to me. We walked down the long corridor and went through the emergency exit and down the stairs. Seconds later he pushed me towards the neck and grabbed me by the throat. Apparently, this motherfucker has a hand problem. He asked me what the fuck was up with me and I played stupid. Didn't I warn this nigga that if he put his hands on me again that I would shoot him? I brushed past him and went outside. After retrieving my bag from the truck, I decided to break all the rules by talking to this sexy ass green eyed Jamaican, pissing Jesse off once again.

We walked back up the hallway stairs and he mumbled that I was either stupid or brain dead. That comment stuck in my head and it was at that moment that I decided to act a jackass. I am determined to kick it up a notch as soon as we get back to Roxy's house. You see, I have never been one to handle rejection well. I sat and listened to him claim to his wife that I was nothing but a sister to him. Oh yeah? Well, correct me if I am wrong but siblings don't do the shit we did the night before. Jesse entered the house first and went straight to Rodney's room.

I sat on the couch and waited for Roxy to come out and show me where I was sleeping. She said that I could bunk in her room. Oh yeah? Issa party party! She trying to get fucked. That is a clear invitation to the pussy. Here it is her husband is her after months on the road and she invites little ole' me to sleep in her bed.

Ain't nobody finna sleep, fuck wrong with her? Jesse came out and announced that he would be sleeping in his son's room as if we gave a fuck. I am so glad that I have all my gear because there was no way that I could lay beside all that ass and not beat. We sat on the couch taking shots of liquor and talking shit. Three shots later, Roxy asked if I was coming on to her. There is something about alcohol that makes a person courageous. Before I could reply, she said that she did not mind my advances.

She just wanted to feel loved for the night. Oh bitch! Love is my middle name. all I needed to know was if the bitch was clean and std free. Some sexually transmitted diseases do not have a look. Next time a person says, thank God I do not look like what I been through, please think twice. She said she was clean and went a step further to show me the results of her last test. Technology is truly amazing! You can keep up with all your health records and appointments with an app on your smart phone. Jesse came back out of Rodney's room and said he was going to take a shower in the master bathroom. I had no idea that this little apartment had two bathrooms. Roxy and I got the impression that he did not like us bonding the way that we were. Roxy said, "Okay, and? You're not in jail anymore Jess, you don't have to announce your every move". He went into her bedroom and slammed the door. We laughed and that prompted her to ask me what his deal was.

Playing stupid while under the influence was not my forte. I shrugged my shoulders and said, "Oh girl, I don't know, he's been crabby for about a week now". She went on to explain that's about how long it has been since he said he wanted a divorce. She said she was okay with that because she wasn't into him anymore. She had only been hanging in there for Rodney, who by the way, looks nothing like him. That's another story and in the words of *Lil' Wayne, "I'm no storyteller"*. Roxy rolled up a blunt and sat in between my legs. I could not resist rubbing her head as we got higher than *Times Square*. Jesse came out and we were cackling like two old hens. I got up and told her that I was going to take my shower. She asked if she could join and before thinking, I said yes. She ran to the back to grab her candles and crystals.

I love that shit! It has been ages since I had a spiritual bath. I was overdue for one. Roxy ran the water and threw in the salts before grabbing an unopened bottle of champagne from the fridge in her room. She really knows how to set the mood. I was impressed by her craftiness. She placed the candles and crystals around the tub and sink before stripping down to her birthday suit. I took my clothes off and asked if she had a speaker that I could connect to Bluetooth with. Of course, she did, so I turned on *Princess Nokia* and got into the water.

We drank and laughed the evening away. Jesse heard the commotion and came into the bathroom to see what was going on. Shocked, he asked what the fuck we were on. Roxy said, "what does it look like, soon to be ex-husband? We are bathing and enjoying each other's company'. I sat back and smirked at Jesse as I sipped my champagne. He said, "No, but while you two are catching up, don't forget to tell her what happened last night". He walked out of the bathroom and slammed the door. Total bitch move! Females do that shit when they want attention. It boggled my mind why he was so mad. He was acting like a sore loser and it was such a turn off. Does he want the bitch or not? The mixed signals ain't it. Roxy asked what he meant, and I downplayed everything.

"Look Ma, we were driving yesterday and decided to stop to get something to eat. He walked into the restaurant first and when I came in, I saw a woman flirting with him. When he saw me, he said, "Oh, there's my wife now". Then he kissed me. I swear to you it was nothing more than that. Roxy straddled my lap and asked if he kissed me like this and began kissing me and biting my bottom lip. This is one feisty bitch. We are making out in the tub and the water splashed everywhere. Neither one of us cared.

Her kisses were passionate, and I was curious to know what the head felt like. If it was not as good as Jesse's, then I would just ask her if he could join in. He is in his feelings, so I know he's going to give us that angry dick. Roxy got out of the tub first and put on a cute lingerie piece. I sleep nude so after I got out, I pranced around in my birthday suit. She laid back on the bed as I put *Donald Glover* on the speaker, loud enough to drown out the noises that she was about to make. I do not mean to toot my own horn; or maybe I do, but I'm the shit in the bed. I come with a mean stroke game. Be it with a man or a woman, I put in work and they are always satisfied. The lights are off, and the candles are burning. I told Roxy to lay on her stomach so that I could rub her body down in my own concoction of natural body butter. As I rubbed her down, I noticed she moaned softly when I got to certain areas on her body. The inner thighs were her sweet spot. Duly noted. When it came time to grease the front of her body; Roxy had wrapped her legs around me so that I was pinned in between her legs. I said, "Damn baby, no foreplay huh? Just jump right into it". I arched my back and ate from her garden. She was already dripping and that boggled my mind. She tasted like fruity water. My job is to devour her so that when I am gone, she yearns for me. That's what I do.

I moved my tongue to the beat of the music for about five or six songs. She dug her nails into my shoulder when I traced my name on her pussy lips with my tongue and gently suckled her clitoris. Her moans were so seductive. Good God! Every time that she was about to cum, she arched her back and dug her nails into my shoulders or arms. Whenever she would yell out; "Oh God, I'm about to cum, I would slide my tongue inside her opening and slurp her juices like I was drinking a thick milkshake from a straw. Drove her nuts and made her quiver. Let us pause for a minute. Ladies why do you yell out for God when you are being sexually satisfied? It has always been weird to me. I had her and it wasn't shit that anyone could do about it. Let me be clear; I am confident, not cocky, there is a difference. Roxy wanted to perform oral sex on me and as curious as I was, I declined her offer. Her husband was nose deep in it last night. I got up and asked her if she was ready for the finishing act and she said of course. It's a damn good thing that I traveled with my gear. If you don't know what that means, then shame on you. I will do my best to explain it to the readers that has lived under rocks. Girl on girl sex requires tools and some of which needs to be assembled. Since lesbians do not come equipped with a cock, we must purchase them.

Pink Cherry is my to go spot for all the kinky toys. I have this killer pair of lime green and black pair of harness boxer briefs. You know? The kind with the O ring in it so that you can slide your dildo through. I pulled out my eight-inch dick that I named *The Donald*. Truth be told, I am obsessed with Mr. Glover and every now and again I will pull him out. All my dicks have a suction cup base so I would stick it to the shower wall or on the lid of a toilet sit and go for a ride while imagining Mr. Glover. Sick right? Judge your mother, not me! Fuck you! These niggas ain't loyal. Montez proved that already. Anyhow, after sanitizing *The Donald* and slipping him into my harness briefs, I got back into the game. I swear to you, I was like a kid on the sideline begging the coach to put him in the game. Just give me one chance and I bet I make you a believer. All the freak came out the both of us. I broke shawty's back, no lie! Just when I thought shit could not get any better, Roxy revealed to me that she had hand and foot restraints attached to her bed. ISSA PARTY! When I have sex with women, I like for it to be missionary.

There is something about watching their ugly sex faces that turns me on. Roxy had no idea what I was capable of. Never underestimate us short people. There really are hidden jewels in small packages. She was gasping for air and digging her nails into my back as I deep stroked her. This bitch acting like she ain't had no dick in a brick and here I am, knocking her pussy loose. At the rate I am going, eventually I will wanna fuck her in the ass. Every time a different song came on, I unleashed some new tricks. I have this signature move where I swivel my waist and hips and stir the pussy up like a bowl of cake batter. You would have to close your eyes to visualize that move. Do you see it? Right on then! It drove her nuts and she came back to back. Roxy licked the sweat off my face and neck. Shortly after, I flipped her over onto her stomach. I'm about to go deeper and tear that ass up the right way. She wasn't ready! I stood behind her, stroking as I caught my breath and waited for the next song to come on. *Redbone by Childish Gambino* came on. It's a slow song to fuck to but I did not bother skipping it. I just stroked to the rhythm. I reached behind me for my phone one minute before the song went off, switching to the *Kevin Gates* station. It was time to murder some shit. After three songs I was tired, and she was trembling like a butt naked hooker in the middle of a snowstorm. Job well done Nicole!

She grabbed me, kissing and caressing my body. I knew she needed me. Energy does not lie. She fell asleep instantly. I washed off and went into the living room to roll a blunt. Jesse was there and he was not happy. Of course, he had heard Roxy moaning and screaming as I dug deep in her guts. Now I wonder if she had been that loud to get his attention. My assumption was that Jesse was jealous. No fucks were given, not by me anyway. As soon as I lit the blunt, Jesse asked me if I thought that what I did was appropriate. Here it is, the middle of the night and I could sense this guy about to pour his heart out to me. I thought he knew me by now. I am heartless! The old Nicole died when I caught my first body. I am a survivalist now and I have no problem ending anyone that got in my way. How dare he sit in my face and question me like I am a child. Was he stupid or just brain dead? I asked Jesse how he wanted things to play out. If he wanted to work things out with his wife, I was cool with that. For all I care, we can part ways now. If he wanted all of us to be one big happy family, I was cool with that too. Let me be clear, I am not attached to a fucking soul. It was just sex to me; a way to release my frustrations. He seemed unsure of what he wanted so I said, "Okay Jesse, tell you what, I'll just find my own way. I have been enough of a burden to you and your family, so I'll roll out as soon as the sun rises". He shook his head as if he agreed with me. This was bound to happen sooner or later. Having sex with the wife he came to New York to divorce had nothing to do with it.

Before I could say another word, I looked up and noticed Roxy standing by the kitchen. She looked disgusted and confused. Roxy asked what was going on and I told her. She said that she didn't want me to leave and that she wanted Jesse to go. That offended him and he felt the need to speak on who I really was. Jesse turned to Roxy and said, "Before you think this bitch is your knightess in shining armor, let's get some things clear. She has killed two people and nearly killed her own husband in the past few months. Nicole is the reason that I haven't been home. I've been helping her clean up her mess. I do not know if she told you the full extent to what happened last night, but baby, we had sex. It was a foolish thing to do and I regret it terribly. I was just confused and lonely. So much had taken place over the last few months and you and I became distant. I would like to work on my marriage. I will find a job in town and promise to never drive across the state line again. You need to understand that when I said that I didn't love you, I was just saying it out of anger and frustration".

Roxy stood in the living room, floored. I am sure a million thoughts went through her head. Seconds had passed and she was speechless. I broke the silence by saying, "Wow, so this is what it's like when you sing the blues? There are not too many men that I know of that runs their mouths like bitches. How much have you had to drink? What were you hoping to accomplish? When we were in Canada you said that you were coming here for a divorce. Now you are singing a different hymn. Tell me what it is, do you feel less of a man knowing that a woman satisfied your wife? What happened to all that shit you said to me? Just last night, you were in love with me. Now you have a change of heart. You know what I will do to anyone that crosses me. At this point, I am feeling crossed". There was no doubt that trust had been broken. Drunken words are sober thoughts so therefore I don't need to process anything. After all that was said, Roxy still asked Jesse to leave. The argument intensified and living room objects were thrown. This is not my fight, so I sat down and watched. Roxy yelled out for Jesse to leave or she would stab him. Now, there is a sight! I would love to see that because he had already run his mouth too much. To make matters worse, she told him that Rodney was not his son. His father was very active in his life and would be here tomorrow to get him. That set Jesse off and he lunged at her. He put both of his hands around Roxy's neck as I stood back, watching in excitement.

Roxy managed to drive a knife through Jesse's chest, and he let her go out of shock. I begged Roxy not to kill him because I didn't know how to drive his truck. She said that she knew how to drive it and would take me anywhere I needed to go as long as I agreed to help her hide his body and let her go on the run with me. An interesting proposal. I agreed and she grabbed him by the hair and sliced his neck. A clean cut might I add. Jesse bled out and died in the living room. Roxy looked unbothered and asked me to roll another blunt while she poured us some shots. She appeared to be still running on adrenaline. We talked about when and how we could move the body, where I needed to head to next. More importantly, she wanted to know if I would betray her. I wanted to know if she would betray me as well. I am all out of people to call my friend. Our only task was to get Jesse out of a tower building before Rodney woke up. Jesse had told me to never use the elevator in the building and I wondered why so I asked Roxy. She said it was the way the dope boys moved their weight and disposed of the bodies of customers that felt like they could skip payments. Anyone that they thought were a threat to their operation would take a one-way trip on the elevator.

All we had to do was give these guys a substantial amount of money and they would help us take out the trash. I think that is a genius idea. Roxy's door is right beside the elevator so no one would see any activity. Three thousand dollars was enough for three guys to help us. One guy, that calls himself Rocco, bust all the lights on Roxy's floor. The neighbors knew not to come out of their units when the hall lights were out. Two other guys; Ken and Tonio, came in to wrap Jesse's body and dragged him onto the elevator. We all crammed on the elevator and went down to the basement floor. After passing the boiler room, I was shocked to find a room with an incinerator in it. What in the fuck goes on in this building? It was unbelievable. All that needed to be done was to clean up Roxy's apartment. Roxy and I went outside to the truck so that I could get some more of my belongings. We walked into the building and approached the stairwell. Rocco yelled out, "Yo, y'all going upstairs right? C'mon, y'all can ride up with me".

He was either attracted to me or Roxy. Nice looking young guy but his choice in work terrified me. Roxy went into her apartment first, leaving Rocco and I standing in the dark hallway. He let me know that he was interested in me. I got a glimpse of his face when we moved the body to the basement and that was the same dude that I pulled my gun on when I first approached the building. He could sense the fear in me and said, "don't trip Ma, that shit was mad sexy, we good". According to him, he knew we would cross paths again. He knew the body that we incinerated was that of Jesse. Before turning to walk away, he said that he wanted to hear that story and handed me his number.

I walked into the apartment to see Roxy on the couch crying. Aww shit, please tell me that this bitch is not regretting the role that she played in all of this. If push came to shove, it was her that killed Jesse, not me. She sat up to pour me a drink and asked if I hit it off with the guy in the hallway. We began to clean the mess and shortly after, Rodney woke up to use the bathroom and ask where his dad was. I told him that Jesse had to do a drop off in

New Jersey and would be back tomorrow morning. That bought us enough time because according to Roxy, Rodney's real father would be picking him up in the morning. We drank liquor, smoked weed and talked about our next move. She confessed that she did not know how to drive the truck; she said that out of anger. Here we are with a truck and no driver. If Roxy could not drive the truck, then she would serve me no purpose. I already was uneasy coming in and seeing her cry over that nigga.

It's a great chance that if we got caught, she would squeal on me and everyone that helped us out in our time of need. That is the thing about collateral damage. Roxy do not know it yet, but tonight is her last night. She is gonna join her husband soon enough. I am more at ease knowing that Rodney would have one parent. She drank herself into a coma and at about three in the morning, I texted the number that Rocco gave me asking for him to meet me in the hallway.

He flew up the elevator! Maybe he thinks that I am expressing interest in him. He texted saying that he was in the hallway and I stood up quietly and exited the door. Rocco smiled as I walked out and said, "Yo, whad up baby gangsta"? I smiled and quietly said, "how much to handle another small problem"? He laughed and said, "Yo Ma, I already knew it would come down to this. Baby girl looked like she was bugging the whole time. This one on us because we gotta cover our ass. It was gon happen anyway, regardless of what you said. We were gon kick the door in and shoot ya shit up but since you came to me and see what we've seen, I'll vouch for you". I am lost for words and all I can do is stare at Rocco in confusion. If I had my gun on me, I would shoot him and take my chances getting out the building and driving the truck myself. How hard can it be? I broke my silence and said, "Just get it done, she's on the couch asleep now. She's waiting for her sons' father to come and pick up her son". Rocco wanted to know what time he would be here, and I said by eight in the morning. He told me that they would wait until tonight. Rocco said that I had to remain with Roxy until they came to handle their business.

There was a knock at the door shortly before eight a.m... Roxy was still passed out, so I opened it and seen a tall dark-skinned man that resembled Rodney. He gave a short introduction before walking to the back to get his son and damned if his name was not Rodney too. There are a lot of secrets going on under this roof. Before leaving, he said, "tell that bitch that Jr. won't be back". In my head; I am like good, because she will be dead soon enough. Hours had passed by as Roxy slept and before I knew it, it was minutes to three. She finally rose from the dead to empty her bladder. When she came out, I let her know that Rodney's dad had come by to pick him up. I did not bother to relay the message that I was told to give her. There was no need to add on to her stress.

She wanted to have sex and I did too. Anything to pass time and take my mind off what was about to happen. We went to the bedroom and did not come out until the sun was down. I went into the kitchen to grab a bite to eat. Roxy went to take a shower and while she was in there, Rocco texted me. I just wanted to get this shit out the way and get on with my itinerary. Roxy came out and asked what time we would be leaving, and I told her to pack her stuff and put it near the elevator. It was about nine o'clock when Rocco texted me again, this time saying "TIME".

We walked to the elevator and Rocco was standing their like concierge. He played things off so smooth and neither of us were suspicious; offering to help put our things in the truck and telling us the safest way to take. We got to the basement floor and before Roxy could ask what was going on, Ken stood behind her with a gun pointed to her back, motioning her to the room with the incinerator in it. She cried and asked me what was going on. I told her that her behavior earlier had upset some people and while she was sleeping, they came to the door, ready to shoot the place up. I begged them to have mercy because her son was asleep in the bedroom.

While I offered her an explanation, Ken grew impatient and shot her in the back of the head. Both Rocco and Ken tossed her into the incinerator while I stood there, lost for words. I had never met people so heartless. Roxy was a liability, but I felt like I could control her. I enlightened them on the situation with the truck and Ken said that I was on my own. I needed to get in the truck, drive off and never return. "Ken, you are one heartless bastard. I don't know anything about driving a truck; so, unless you have some tips on how to drive it or someone to do the driving for me, you might as well toss me in the incinerator too. You're coming at me all hostile, like I did something to you, and I didn't". Even with a gun pointed at my head, I still talked shit. No man puts fear in my heart, and I mean that shit. It's either, he is gonna give me a car to drive and make the truck disappear or he is gonna have someone drive me where I need to go. What he will not do is make me feel bad for not knowing how to drive a truck that professionals drive. Rocco agreed to take me to Pennsylvania so that I could catch up with Aunt Lu.

Chapter 4

LuAnn's Betrayal Exposed

After a four-hour drive, we had finally made it to LuAnn's house. It was a fun road trip. Rocco is so humble and down to earth. He cracked many jokes. He let me know that the number he gave me was for me to use anytime I needed him. He really liked me, although we got off on the wrong foot. Before seeing me off, he got out the car to hand me my bags and give me a hug. I walked into LuAnn's house expecting to be embraced by her and Jenesis. Instead, I walked in to see Aunt Lu shocked by my presence. There was no embrace and we just stood in the middle of the floor waiting for someone to say something. Lu is throwing mad shade, and I am nervous to know what she had to tell me in person.

Jenesis ran downstairs and jumped on me. At least someone is happy to see me. It has been so long since I have seen her. She grew at least three inches and loss a couple of baby teeth. I could hear Messiah and Angel in the next room, so I ran to go see them. After 6 long months I finally got the chance to hold my babies. You cannot even tell they were born early. It felt so good to be near all my children again. I knew the feeling would not last long, so I will cherish this moment forever.

While holding Messiah, I thanked Aunt Lu for taking such good care of them. It is apparent that she loves these kids like they are her own, even though she does not have any. I made small talk about her taking care of me when I was a young girl. The way she brushed my hair was the exact same way Angel's hair was brushed. The more I talked, the more I could see that LuAnn could give a shit less about what I was saying. I wonder what I had done to her. Was leaving my kids in her care a burden to her? Did I do something offensive to her? I wished she would open her mouth and say something instead of keeping me wondering. "Aunt Lu, talk to me baby, we are so much better than this. I consider you as my mother. We have been through hell and back more times than I can count. Please talk to me". She broke her silence by talking about the twins' progress. It is like she was giving me a manifesto. Do you know how a person talks when they know that their time is coming to an end? That is how she sounded!

She told me what the kids like to eat, where they like to play, etc. Then she held her head up; looking me in the eyes and said that she was HIV positive. I looked at her and noticed that she had lost a lot of weight. How long have you known this auntie? Why didn't you tell me sooner? I would have come home a long time ago. Tez got locked up in May 2019, so Aunt Lu did not have any help with the children. I felt horrible! She said that she scraped up bond money for him in August and he came home for about 2 weeks. He was locked up again because the evidence and ballistics pointed to him. Aunt Lu depleted her emergency funds on Tez and the kids. She could not even afford her medications anymore. Luann said that these few months had been extremely hard on her. Detectives had been pressing her out for months. They shut her business down because they figured she knew more than she was telling them. They even went as far as threatening to charge her with obstruction of justice and providing false testimony to the authorities.

She admitted that she finally cracked when the feds threatened to take my children away from her. Her excuse was that, even rocks crumble, eventually. According to LuAnn, the only thing she told the feds was that I had killed Nakyta after she lunged at me with a knife. Deep down I suspected that she was lying, but at this point it does not matter. I am fucked! Do not get me wrong, I understand the position she had been put in, but some shit was not adding up. I know for a fact that I could no longer trust her. As I said before, we have over 30 years secrecy. There's shit that she has done that will never roll off my tongue. There is no such thing as loyalty anymore. I put the press on her, and she finally admitted that she thought Montez deserved better than me. It became clear to me that her and Montez had something going on and I was sick to my stomach. I excused myself and went to take a shower. Boiling hot water ran down my back and I was too numb to feel anything other than heartbreak. Had Aunt Lu been sleeping with my husband? Why would she say those hurtful things to me? Montez started all this shit with his infidelity so what did she mean that he deserved better than me?

I sobbed uncontrollably as anger filled my body. This is the exact same rage that I felt when I shot Montez. You would think that by now, people would tread more lightly with their words. I am a sweet girl and I would give you the shirt off my back on a rainy day, but I am still my father's child. Once I am mad or enraged, there is nothing that I will not do. That was proven months ago. After getting out of the shower and getting dressed, I returned downstairs. Aunt Lu had Messiah in her arms and Jenesis was playing with Angel. They looked like a tight knit family. That is what made me contain my anger. My children had no one. My time here would be short, and I do not know when or if I will ever see them again. Aunt Lu continued where she left off. She blamed me for her losing her business and she blamed me for not being able to control my anger. According to her, all men cheat and our job as women is to look the other way. Is this bitch retarded? Maybe that is her role in a man's life, but that could never be my role.

No way! Was I supposed to dismiss what I had been feeling for the sake of everything that would fall apart? I am a serious believer of, you could have just left me the fuck alone. I did not seek him out. It was the other way around. He could have looked the other way. That's how men are though. They must have the shiny new toy in order to feel whole. Something about needing a notch under their belt. Nonetheless, I wasn't having none of that shit. You do me wrong and I will do you grimy.

LuAnn finally told me that she had an intimate relationship with Montez and that she was in love with him. I had already prepared myself for that news so that I would not act out of impulse. It didn't hurt any less though. Lu said that things just happened after I shot Tez. She was already lonely after her husband died three years ago. It did not help by her going to see about Montez while he was in the hospital and in the rehab facility. That is where her feelings grew. It wasn't until Montez came home, did her feelings get the best of her and they engaged in relations. As hurt as I was to hear that, I understand her vulnerability. I knew that Montez was manipulating her. He was doing this to get to me. A part of him is hurt that I shot him and Nakyta, so he is gonna drive a wedge in between me and the closest thing I have to a mother.

Well played Tez! Good one! Genius! Sloppy as shit. He didn't think things out though. He underestimated me again. I have connections in high places. That's why his ass is locked up now. All the evidence pointed back to me; but when you have friends in law enforcement and forensic labs, results can be easily manipulated, and you remain a force to be reckoned with. It's not even the fact that people can be paid to look the other way. This is about my morals and integrity. I am a good human being. I just got caught up with someone not so good. I really miss Al. He taught me so much. One principle that he lived by was to never let your left hand know what your right hand is doing. I never showed all the cards I was holding, and I believe that is what has been keeping me afloat. To be able to see and feel things before it happens is a true gift. That is an empaths reward.

I knew what Aunt Lu had to tell me when we spoke on the phone and she said she wanted to talk in person. The mind has a hard time grasping certain things even when all the evidence is laid out in front of you. The heart automatically knows, even when you do not want it to. It is always the ones that you think would never do you like that, that does the foulest shit. Al taught me how to remove my feelings from situations. I am not an emotional thinker because of him. Do not get me wrong. I am an emotional person; I just know how to remove my feelings when it comes to life or death situation. It took a moment for me to find words to say to LuAnn. I asked her what I had done to her personally to deserve to be hurt and betrayed in that manner. I wanted to know if it was worth it considering that we had been thick as thieves since I was knee high to a fry.

I made sure that she knew that Montez only entertained her to get under my skin. He doesn't love anyone, especially not her. He fell in love with what she was doing for him. Then it clicked! This bitch said she was

HIV positive. People always say then I am not the sharpest crayon in the box because it takes me awhile to process certain information. I asked Aunt Lu when she found out that she was positive and when she started sleeping with Tez. All kinds of thoughts filled my head. Had Tez and Aunt Lu slept together unprotected? Did Lu infect him, or did he infect her? Am I infected? What else was it that she was not telling me? This whole time I sat in utter silence, letting my thoughts get the best of me. She sat back, observing with a smirk on her face.

"Alright Nicole, I'll tell you everything. You see; I never had children because when I was younger, I was pregnant and had to have an abortion after finding out that I was positive. My husband had been cheating on me with multiple women and cursed me with their disease. Jonny did not die of cancer, he died of AIDS. I took care of him until his last dying breath. I have managed my disease through good dieting and a regimen of medications. I didn't bother trying to move on because I was ashamed of my status".

Here I sat, sympathizing with my aunt and feeling sorry for her when she said that there was more that she had to tell me.

"After Jonny passed away, I found out that Nakyta was his niece. I knew all about the relationship between Nakyta and Montez. They had an on and off thing for some years. They even have a set of twins together; I believe they are eight by now. Nakyta's mother is raising the twins now. Montez's mother helps as well. Montez has been lying to you this whole time and I did not say anything because I knew how much you loved him. I didn't want to be the one to hurt you. He has been legally married to Nakyta for four years up until you killed her. Montez and I paid a preacher to perform a wedding for you because you kept pressuring him to marry you. I have been telling Montez to tell you the truth ever since him and Nakyta hooked back up in 2018.Just days after you two married, Nakyta found out and threatened to reveal the truth. As far as Montez and I go, as I said, things just happened. We started off using protection; but when I realized that he was trying to manipulate and mind fuck me, it reminded me of Jonny's lies and deceit. It became personal to me. I blamed him for Nakyta's death even though it was at your hands. I blamed him for your absence, and it disturbed me that he could be so callous with people's heart.

Montez was infected by me and he knew about it. I told him almost immediately and he still chose to sleep with you when you came back the first time. Maybe my actions were wrong, but I do not feel sorry and will not apologize. Your mother will be upset with me when I talk to her, but I will explain the situation. There ain't shit she can do anyway. Your best bet is to go ahead and start treatment because if the two of you did anything unprotected, then you are infected. Everything that he has done to you has been payback for you killing his wife and shooting him. There is no more explaining that I can do. Nothing I say will change the facts or bring you comfort. I'm open to answer questions that you may have, but keep in mind that I too was a victim to Montez's shit".

There are no words that I can find to explain how I am feeling. What is sad is that someone I consider a mother could be so careless and disregard my feelings like she is doing. Betrayed is beyond what I am feeling. My heart hurts so bad. Tears flowed down my eyes and landed on my chest. Numbness, all I feel is numbness! The last two years of my life has been a lie. All I wanted to know was, why? Why would she feel the need to shatter my world the way that she just did? I don't believe that out of all the people in the world, she would be the one to break my heart the way that she did. Jonny cheating on her could have been the start of her anger towards men. What exactly was her issue with me though? So, I asked, "Why me"?

LuAnn replied,

"Back in 1990, I had started dating Jonny, Things were going smooth and then I found out that he had been sleeping with my sister, your mother. I was devastated to learn this and even more hurt to learn that your sister was the love child produced in the mix. We had no idea that we were dealing with the same man until after Boobie gave birth and I asked about the child's father. When I found out that Jonny was the father, I waited until the baby turned two months old and suffocated her in her sleep. That must've been in late '91. Then she met your father and got pregnant with you. Your mom received false information as to how your sister died and as a result, she killed two people that she thought was responsible. She gave birth to you while in prison and I decided to raise you as my own. I raised you out of guilt for what I had done to my sisters' first child. Looking back, I guess you can say that I had a personal beef to settle. Things backfired in my face and here we are".

This was and has never been about me. She chose to hurt me because she felt betrayed by my birth mother. A woman that I do not even know. One thing is for sure, family is messy. It's 2020 and this bitch is still trying to settle a score from 1992. She is playing God and enjoying every moment of it. How much can you hate another individual to be willing and able to kill an innocent child? I am trying to picture the conversation that would take place between my mother and Lu. What has gotten into LuAnn? Where did the sudden disregard for her family start? Looking in hindsight, I do remember family tell me that, she only knows you when she needs something. That is the only time you are relevant. I have never seen her so callous, or maybe I chose not to. In all my years of knowing her, she has always been sweet and caring to everyone's needs. She pretended so well. I stood; staring into LuAnn's eyes, in disbelief by everything I had to process and then the phone rings.

[LuAnn answers the phone and puts it on speaker]

There is an automated operator on the other end trying to connect a prepaid prison call. It's MON-FUCKING-TEZ! How convenient. My day just keeps getting better.

"Hey baby, just calling to check on my leading lady and the kids. How is everything on that end? Any news about my next court date? How is everything on that end? Have you heard from their mother? Will you move forward with adopting all the kids? BABE?? Why are you so quiet"?

LuAnn says, "Tez, the kids are fine; very busy and always hungry. I am still in need of my medication. The lawyer called two days ago and removed himself from your case at my request. You are scheduled for court sometime next year. He said that the judge decided to push the case back and I did not see the need to keep paying him for nothing. There is something that I need to tell you. I haven't been completely honest with you, just as you have not been honest with me. Let me start by saying that I do love you. You know that I do not have much time. This disease has advanced, and I am down to my last few months. Do you remember when we slept together, and I asked If you wanted to go through with it considering that I was HIV positive "?

Montez says, "Yes, well what are you getting at? What is going on? You are talking like it is the end of the world, and we still have plenty living to do. Why do you think that I refuse to marry Nicole? I love you LuAnn".

LuAnn says, "Tez STOP! The jig is up! I know you've lying and manipulating me just to extort money from me. Long story short, the judge is removing you from protective custody status, so you will be sent into general population sometime this week. He also pushed to have you transferred to Noakwood Correctional Facility. Supposedly, they have proof that you conspired to kill Nakyta and that you had killed Al. I do not know what else to do at this point, so I am washing my hands of the situation. This is all your fault! Had you just been honest and told Nicole that you and Nakyta were married, none of this shit would be happening".

He goes on to say, "Is that right? So, you turning your back on me too? Do you even remember why I am in protective custody? Lu, I was gang raped and beaten by three men in here. You are gonna send me back to that? Why would they send me back in population when I had already agreed to tell them everything they wanted to know about Nicole"?

And then I said, "Is that right Montez? What exactly is it that you know about me baby? How does your ass feel dada? I warned you that if you played with fire, you would eventually get burned. HIV! You gave me HIV? You have been playing me all along eh? Sleeping with my aunt, were you? Unprotected, did you? You knew she was infected and still chose to sleep with me unprotected while I carried your kids. Are the twins infected too? That is a low blow baby! All things considered; I am not mad and perhaps that is not a good thing. A bogus marriage though? You done fucked up for real! It's always love on my end. Keep your head up, eyes open and booty hole closed. God be with you baby"!

Before ending the call, LuAnn told Tez that she was sorry that she was sorry that things turned out this way and that she had told me everything. I demanded that she give me the keys to one of her cars in the garage. Minutes later, I went upstairs to pack all the kid's clothes. I loaded everything in the car and strapped the twins in their car seat. Jenesis began to cry and I told her that I would explain things in the car. I'm not a bamma ass bitch and I do understand that Lu loved my kids, so before driving off, I let her say her goodbyes. After that was all said and done, I told LuAnn that I was dead to her. There was no coming back from that level of betrayal. For the first time, in a long time, I seen LuAnn break down and cry. She offered me an apology and asked that I leave my kids in her care. They are all she has according to her. I know how to get under her skin now, and this time I will not let up. She needs to hurt and suffer. Taking my kids would kill her faster than the AIDS virus. I got in the car and backed out of the driveway as she ran towards the car. The same smirk she gave me while revealing her betrayal; was the same smirk I gave her as I drove off.

FUCK HER AND MONTEZ!

CHAPTER 5

<u>MONTEZ'S FATE</u>

Montez has backstabbed and betrayed a lot of people; and as a result, he sits at Orakee Correctional Facility, awaiting sentencing. No one knows if a transfer or sentencing will come first. He is at Orakee, terrified of the last conversation he had with Nicole. Montez had been locked up for exactly one month since Lu last bailed him out. In that month, he had been sexually violated. You are probably wondering why and how he ended up in that position. A wise reader would wonder, who is telling this part of the story. Well; I do not want to add on to your suspense, so allow me to introduce myself. My name is Devin; and I am the man that violated Montez and made him my personal bitch. Oh bitch, let me give you the tea!

Life throws you some curve balls that I find to be interesting. One minute, you are an innocent child, defending yourself against bumble bees and baseballs; to an adult, defending yourself from random gunshot violence and prison bids. As I mentioned before, my name is Devin, a.k.a. Devo. I am serving a ten-year bid for armed robbery. I've been down for three years and change. Shortly before, my girl at the time gave birth to my daughter. When I first got to Orakee, I was ganged raped by three big and aggressive men. The things they did to me was indescribable. As time went on, I learned that it was something that happened to every man that set foot in this institution. It's either you gave in to the demands of horny and backed up men; or you took your chances fighting for your manhood. Nine times out of ten, you would end up losing your life in the most gruesome way. I have seen it with my own eyes. Honey, listen. About two years ago, my friend Darius was killed because he chose to fight for his manhood. Now I do not know why he did not want to give that booty hole up because we had a thing for a few months. God rest his soul... until I get there.

Anyway chile...

As I was saying, for about two and a half years, I tried to fight these men's off; but they insisted that they would help turn me into the person I was meant to be. Try to picture a five-foot four-inch caramel complexion man with long curly hair, fighting five to six giant size men, three times a week for two years. Hell, even rocks crumble. God did not come through for me. I fit every man's type when it comes down to it. Little did they know, I enjoyed being fucked in the ass. Before I got here, I was in a relationship with my baby mother. She introduced me to my true self.

I used to be ashamed of the things that she would do to me in the bedroom; until I was gang raped in this hell hole by three men. Two men that stood at six foot – eight inches tall. They had to be twins. I will not get into much detail. Just know that within a month of me being here, they got ahold of me in the shower room. Two held me down while the other would ram his dick down my throat until he nutted. Then the other would pick me up and forcibly bounce me up and down his dick until he exploded in my ass. They were expecting that first-time fear and terror that a newbie would have after having dicks rammed in them aggressively, for the first time. Not me baby. You see that shit made my dick hard. Surely if they had bother sucking me off, they would see how into it I was. They should have taken note by the way I would throw my ass back on their dicks while they called themselves raping me. It felt good to me and it reminded me of the way Nicole would fuck me. Damn I miss that girl.

I am sure you are imagining how in the hell I know Nicole. Well dig it! We had a five-year relationship and then I got into some trouble. She was pregnant when I got locked up. I never got to meet my daughter and I never heard from Nicole once I got sentenced. Back in our day, we were something like swingers. Nicole was attracted to women and into dominatrix styled sex. I loved to see her in action with them. It kept our relationship lively. As little as she was, she owned me in the bedroom. I would dress up in wigs and high heels and prance around the house. I would even crawl around to show my submission to her. She would allow me to bend over and would fuck me with an eight- inch realistic cock while I called her, "Mistress". Tore my ass up, but I loved it. It made me cum hard. Things slowed down when she found out that she was pregnant. It's like, she did not have it in her to satisfy me anymore. She wanted to fly straight and set an example for our kid. Never mind how good she made me feel. I get it now, but back then, I needed the feeling that she gave me.

I will never forget the first night it happened. We had left a concert at Capital Arena in DC. She boasted and bragged about how much I resembled the artist performing. It must have been *Childish Gambino* that performed, because that's the only artist that she would pay to see. Anyhow, she was feeling her drinks and in a state of euphoria. She was riled up because the performer walked off the stage and let her tell it, he stopped the show and walked the halls and walk down the section she was sitting at. He stopped to smile at her and hold her hand while she screamed and hollered like the true fan that she was. I love Nicole's arrogance. She knew she was the shit baby! We got home that night and she grabbed me by my neck and demanded that I call her Mistress. I am feeling my drinks and I gave into her. She took off her wig and put it on my head, while demanding that I eat her pussy. Fuck it! I agreed.

WARNING! WARNING! WARNING!

This part of the story takes a different turn. It may be offensive to straight men and I apologize in advance. This shit really happened, and I would be lying to myself if I did not include everything. Feel free to skip to the next chapter because these next few pages will be lit.

Nicole straddled my face without warning as I sat on the couch. I slid down to get more comfortable while she gyrated on my face as the songs came on and went off. She would look down at me with the most seductive eyes in the world and demand that I slurp her juices from her hole as she orgasmed. "Mistress! permission to drink from your well", is what she would make me say. I knew when she would cum because she always demanded that I grab her by the neck and choke her. Nicole had this toy called the Womanizer. She would make me sit in a corner, chained to a dog leash; watching her get her nuts off as she yelled out things like, "You're a pitiful bitch, a horrible lover, you could never fuck me as good as I could fuck you". She said that she couldn't wait to fuck me like the pretty little bitch that I was. She wanted to teach me how to lay pipe correctly. Shit, now I'm curious to know exactly what she means; so, I yelled out, "I'm your little bitch, Mistress. Give me some dick"! Nicole flew to the bedroom and within two minutes; she came out, dressed in a black Nike sports bra and black briefs with a purple dick hanging out. She told me to get down on my knees and crawl over to her. She wanted me to beg to taste her dick and I did.

I begged, "Mistress please", before she gave in. I licked up and down her shaft while she leaned back on the wall biting her bottom lip and cupping my head. She said, "ooohhh, you're my little bitch. I'm gonna put you in heels and fuck the lining out of you". She snatched her dick out of my mouth and walked to the bedroom. I went back into the corner and waited until "Mistress" returned. She came back with a six-inch pair of pink stiletto boots and demanded that I put them on and assume the position. She stood near the couch, rubbing her hands together and eagerly waiting for me to get both shoes on. Y'all I looked up and seen her stroking her dildo as if it was really her dick. This bitch does too much! I walked over to her and before I could say or do anything, she dropped to her knees and began topping me off. One minute later, she got up and said, "Now that is how you suck a dick"! She stood up, grabbing me by the neck and bending me over. I spread my butt cheeks apart and she began eating my ass and sticking her tongue, in and out of my hole.

Before I knew it, she would manage to get two fingers in my ass. It hurt and felt good at the same time. She moved her fingers in and out and pulled me back by my waist until I began sliding back on her fingers myself. I gasped because it felt good enough to cum. Nicole is a connoisseur of male anatomy. She used her finger to locate the male g-spot and let me know exactly how far up my ass it was. When she seen that I had erupted, she flogged me four times and pushed my face into the semen that hit the floor. "EAT IT", she screamed! Nicole came up behind me and grabbed me by the waist as I sat on my knees and hands eating my own specimen from the floor. She got down on her knees and eased her dick inside my hole. Her long passionate strokes felt so magical. Anything Nicole wanted from me; I was happy to oblige. That's how affectionate and convincing she is. I was hard as a bone and ready to cum. She threatened to flog me again if I did anything without her permission. Her moves are mesmerizing. Regardless of what song that comes on, she is always on beat. It is like she is the soul that flows through the music playing.

She tossed me on my side and stroked my dick, while still inside my ass, until I exploded. While I was nutting, she was banging my backout. Moving forcefully and doing all kinds of tricks. I guess she was upset that I got off. I shrieked, gasped and screamed. She would not let up. I tried to push her off me, but she had me pinned on my side, and I could not move one bit. She saw that I was overly excited, so she pulled out and looked at me seductively. Before I could say anything, she rammed her dick inside of me. Every inch she packed was in me. She pumped and pumped until I screamed out, "FUCK ME"! It felt so good to see this small woman handle a grown ass man. My legs were pinned in the air. One of her hands was on the side of my waist and the other was wrapped around my ankles as they were suspended in the air. She started to slow down and began reaching for my hand. She put my hand around her neck and said, "Daddy choke me"! I did that until she came and when she was done, she stood up and rammed her dick down my throat and said, "DON'T FUCKING TOUCH ME"! She got up, without saying a word; just like a nigga would. So masculine and feminine at the same time. I recommend everyone get them a Nicole in their life.

Fast forward to how I know Montez. I was out on bond and awaiting trial when I met Montez. He seemed like a cool cat. I would see him on the block, always about his business. He did not keep a large crowd around him, and he was low key. Never wore flashy shit or drove flashy cars. He did not even play loud music. I started buying weed from him just to feel him out. After learning how much time I would have to serve, I made him a business deal he could not refuse. I offered to pay him twenty-five thousand dollars a year to drive Nicole around and keep an eye out for her and the baby. Montez is tall and handsome, but he also looks like someone you ought not fuck with. When I learned that he had broken the code by dating and having sex with her, my heart broke. On top of all that, this nigga got my bitch pregnant. Foul on top of foul. That sent me into a rage. Nicole was untouchable. He violated in every way possible. My dick got hard for him. All I could think was that I would one day violate him too. As luck would have it, Montez would get locked up and sent here, to Orakee. Karma worked out in my favor and I was determined to initiate him.

Let me explain how that goes. The prison put bids in on incoming inmates. Whoever got the most money, can choose from any fish coming in. I say fish because they squirm like fishes when they are being fucked. I waited for days to reveal myself, while he walked around the joint with his head held high and chest poked out. I studied his moves and watched who he associated with before I showed my face to him. I had paid three men to snatch Tez out of the rec room and bring to the shower room. When he got there; he looked terrified, like he had seen a ghost. He was shocked to see me and how much I had changed. I wore a stuffed bra and had makeup on with my hair in curls and a bun. Not the Devo he remembers. I explained to Montez that he had fucked up. He said, "And what your bitch ass gone do about it. Look at you man. Does Nicole know this shit"? I said, "You had one job Montez, ONE"! Tez could not control his hormones and as a result my girl is on the run. Even though, Nicole is out there, and I am in here; I still get information. I have helped Nicole as far as my money would allow me and she does not even know it. She thinks that I just walked away from the relationship.

After what happened to me, I assumed that she would never be able to be with me.

I paid the judge to push Montez's trial back and have him sent to Noakwood. I'm going to have my way with him and send him to Nicole's father when I am done. He sat, on his knees, waiting for me to say something. I just looked at him because I already knew what I was about to do to him. As small as I am, I have a really big dick. It is easily nine inches long and girthy. Montez said, "So what's up Devo, you are looking mad different from what I can remember. What's up baby? I know you not still mad about that situation with Nicole". I circled around him and said, "Tez Tez Tez, it's so good to see you baby. I'm so glad you are here. No hard feelings about you getting my girl pregnant and starting all that wild shit in her life. I told you that she was untouchable". I asked him about the relationship he had with her because if it was anything like ours; she had already fucked him. I knew how he felt about gay men from back in the hood. He would always talk shit whenever one would walk by.

The guys that I paid to act as my muscle, had pinned Tez to the wall near the shower stall and I dropped to my knees in front of him. He looked scared, even begged me to stop with the gay shit. He squirmed, fussed, and cussed when I took his dick out his pants. I said, "Oh, I see why Nicole couldn't get enough of you. Look how thick your dick is". I licked the head and the head only and he got hard as a bone. He began trying to fight but my muscles were not having it. I began sucking his dick and massaging his balls. When I started deep throating him, he let out a soft moan. He couldn't resist the warmth of my mouth. I can tell he liked sloppy head because while I was deep throating him, he took his hand and pushed my head further down on his dick. He closed his eyes and for a moment, forgot that I was a man. I certainly did not look like one. Now I am angered by his reaction because all I could see is him doing this to Nicole. I got up and asked him if this was the way he did my woman. His dick went soft and he began putting up a fight. My men bent him over and I let him know to shut the fuck up and take this dick. I slapped him on the ass a few times and began licking his ass. He loved that shit! Especially when I shoved my tongue in his asshole. I licked and licked; and shoved my middle finger up his ass.

He wanted to be fucked. Anyone with working eyes could see that. His booty hole was tight. There was a slight red tinge when I took my finger out. Nicole had not popped his cherry completely and my dick grew so hard at the thought of getting virgin ass. I was eager but I still took my time easing my dick into his hole. He screamed, cried and begged me to stop. I motioned for one of my muscles to gag him. I pounded and pounded, going deeper and deeper in his ass, the louder he got. He broke my girls' heart and now was the time to break his and much more. I got tired and felt like cumming. Not before I yelled out, "THIS IS FOR NICOLE, BITCH"!

It was time for some fellatio from Tez. My guys put him on his knees, and I let him know that his mouth better feel as good as mines did or all the men in this room would take turns fucking the lining out of him. Two at a time. I shoved my dick in his mouth and he began sucking on it. Man, oh man does this boy know how to suck a dick. His hands were pinned in my muscles arms and he was still handling my dick like a pro. I motioned for my men to turn him loose and I grabbed his head while he wrapped his hands around my ass. I emptied my load down his throat as he gagged. "Mhmmm Mhmm bitch, no teeth. Swallow all that nut", I said. My body twitched in amazement. He was excellent. What he did next surprised me. He sat on the toilet, stroking his bone and motioned for me to come sit on it. I obliged.

As soon as I walked over to him, he sat me down on his dick; and arched his hips upward, lifting me up and down to ride him. I moaned so loud. I bounced up and down and spun around so that we were facing each other. We both panted and I clinched my asshole so tight, he began to shoot his load up my ass. We kissed each other in the mouth passionately. He put up a good fight. Pushing me off him after he nutted and realized I was still a man. I wanted him to hold me and run his long hands through my curly hair; and when that didn't happen, I unleashed one of my muscles on him and left. At the end of the day, I prevailed, and he would be my bitch until his transfer.

Montez laid on the shower floor, bloody and afraid. I am told that the guards came in and rushed Tez to the infirmary. They asked what had happened and no one knew anything. Hours went by and I got word that Montez wanted to see me. The guards escorted me to the infirmary; where I would walk in to see him lying on his stomach, looking pitiful. I got close to him and he said for me to get him out of there. Him being there put him at risk to be raped again. Word travels fast in here. If one inmate saw him then the whole prison did too. They were already putting their bid in for him. I talked to the warden and he agreed to let him go to solitary confinement for one week.

Anything after that, would be up to his family or whoever he had on the outside with money. One week with total privacy with Montez. I would be his only contact person for seven entire days. His ass is pretty banged up, so I couldn't fuck him just yet. He could suck my dick and fuck me though.

I visited him three times a day and got him everything that he needed. Cell phone calls were made by him to get a prolonged stay in solitary confinement. We talked about the shit he had done to land him here; more specifically, we talked about how and why he decided to hook up with my girl. You know I take this shit personal. I am not completely heartless, so I waited until the night of the third day before I began shoving my dick down Tez's throat again. He hated it and I did not care. He would pay every day of his life for the shit that he did to my girl. I would ride him, and he would curse and moan at the same time. He no longer put up a fight or tried to resist my advances. He even began drinking my load with no hesitation. It felt amazing to him and he had nothing else to do. He was too arrogant to thank God for still being alive. I have seen it go both ways in here.

He didn't care much for me riding him face to face at first. Once he laid on his back, he did not mind. I had more range and could ride better. Montez loved when I rode him from the back. He would pull my hair out of its ponytail and scatter it all over my head; choke me and all that. He loved when I would say, "this your pussy daddy", after he would ask whose pussy this was. That was enough to make him erupt in my ass. I must look like a woman from the back because as the days went by, he was all in. It got deep in confinement. Maybe he was looking to pass time or maybe he was afraid. Whenever I was ready to get a nut off, I would go see Tez and put my dick in his mouth. I did not care if he was asleep or in the middle of prayer. My dick went in his mouth a gummy worm and came out, a thick long bone ready to get buried.

On the fifth day of confinement, I went to put my dick near his mouth, and he refused to open up. That stunned me! Now I want some ass. His resistance is turning me on. A fight broke out between the two of us and at first, he had the upper hand. I grabbed him by the dick and head butted him, causing him to collapse onto his left side. I tore the pants from around his waist and rammed my dick so far up his asshole, that I could feel the stitches pop open. He cried! Let out the most painful shriek that I have yet to

Once I got back to the tier that I was housed on. I let everyone know that I had broken Montez and that if anyone wanted a piece of him, they would have to pay me. I would be the least of Montez's worries. These men are bigger and more aggressive and are already putting their bids in. Now I will not lie, I sympathize for any person that has gone through this kind of ordeal. He was not human to me anymore. He played with my family, so I felt that I owed him that. A breaking in gift. I was gentle with him for the most part. The men after me will fuck him to death. Now that everyone knows he has been broken in; he doesn't stand a chance. I also made it a point to contact Nicole after all these years and tell her the news. She was shocked to hear from me but could not thank me enough.

The seventh day did not come because Montez had been transferred shortly after I had left his cell. Word around the jail is that he was sent down to Noakwood. Them cats do not play that. Nicole's father is there. He is serving a life sentence for at least nine murders and some other wild shit. Pops wasn't right back in the day. They say he is reformed, some kind of mentor now. Even if he decides to punk out on standing up for his daughter, I did my part. There is something special about that woman. I will always love her.

CHAPTER 6

<u>DEAL OR NO DEAL!</u>

Montez was sent straight to the medical unit of Noakwood Correctional Facility in Washington DC. For one week, he would lie on his stomach, receiving the best medical care that he could get. It was all a plot for the detectives to get the information they needed on Nicole. No one bothered Tez. He was able to heal in peace before being sent to population. No one knows who he is, and the staff here do not expose people's medical history. The detectives purposely waited until Montez got situated, to begin interviewing him. That's how the feds are! They do not give a hoot about anything but solving a case; in which they are too incompetent to solve on their own, which is why they rely so heavily on witness statements. While Montez was in the chow hall for lunch, two correctional officers came in and escorted him to the wardens' office where two detectives would await him.

Detective Boone introduced herself and Detective Aldez. Boone would go on to let Montez know that she had

heard about his ordeal at Orakee and wanted to help him. Funny ain't it? The broad did not want to help him while he was there and now, she wants to help. Go figure! She began by asking who Nakyta Michaels was to him. Why he had killed her, questions that would upset him into confessing everything. At the end of the day, a man will be a man. We are hunters by nature. It is not that our women do wrong by us or do not know how to please us. We are just.........
hunters by nature.

Montez said, "Nakyta and I had been married for six years and have a set of eight-year-old twins. That woman was my heart. I didn't kill her, and I am torn apart that she is dead. I watched her beg for her life and witnessed her body hit the floor. That was a good woman and mother. She did not deserve to die the way that she did. You know, me and Nakyta had our ups and downs with the profession she chose but I would give her my lungs if that was what she needed. I wish I could take it all back. Go back to the day I saw Nicole and walk the other way. It all started when I began selling weight to her dude. He approached me with an offer, and I accepted it. Figured it to be harmless. I couldn't fuck it up. No one could. He told me he would be going on an extended vacation; said he needed someone to keep an eye on his girl and daughter while he was gone. Things were going well for the first year. I would watch Nicole get on and off the bus with her daughter and she always looked lonely.

One day, I saw her struggling to hold her daughter and groceries, so I offered to help. That short time in her presence had done something to me. Nicole had the most innocent yet seductive eyes that I had ever seen. She spoke fluent and proper English, didn't curse and was very attentive to her child. In the months that I watched her, no one crossed her threshold. She didn't have any visitors. I watched her go to work and come home every day. I would catch a glimpse of her reading to her daughter when she sat on her front porch. My feelings for her intensified and when I noticed that, I had cut off the contract with her dude and stayed away from Nicole. Months would go by before I would see or hear from her again. Things happened and I ended up living two lifestyles. All Nicole wanted was to be loved and for a moment I thought I could do that. I went through things with Nakyta and it pushed me to Nicole. So, I am in a love triangle and got messy at covering my tracks.

As time went on, she told me that she would not have sex again until she was married. She had been through so much and ended up being a single mother. I sympathized with her because deep down inside of me, I knew history would repeat itself. The truth is that I had got caught slipping and instead of me coming clean when Nicole questioned me about it, I chose to lie. One night in a drunken fit, Nakyta had went through my phone and connected all the dots. She was hurt and all I could do was avoid the conversation. She thought that Nicole was just someone that gave me a book to read. Life had taken its course and before I knew it, Nakyta outed me to Nicole. She waited for me to go to sleep and texted Nicole. They conjured up a plan and I was ignorant to the whole thing. Next day, I texted Nicole and she told me to come over. I'm lying in her lap and she went off. Supposedly, there was purple glitter in my hair.

I watched a whirlwind of emotions go through Nakyta and I did not know what to do. I was caught! As nonchalant as I am, I had the nerve to go and take a shower. When I got out, she had shot me and threatened to kill me if I didn't take her to my wife's house. She drove as I sat on the passengers' side, trying not to bleed out. I knocked on the door and Nakyta opened it. Nicole pushed through the door and aimed the gun at Nakyta. She begged for her life before that bitch shot her. My kids' mother is gone man! After that, she drove me to the hospital and pushed me out of the car as it was still moving, then sped away. While in the hospital, I called Al to clean up the situation. I didn't want Nicole to get in trouble. This would have never happened had I just been honest.

There is not a doubt in my mind that she killed Al too. He had turned on her and I know enough about her to know that she lives by the street code. He was a liability. Her aunt LuAnn told me that she also plans on killing the district attorney and judge. She has people in the police department and other places that work for her. She is damn near untouchable. It's like one bad mistake, caused her to go insane. She will not stop until everyone involved is dead, including me. Ain't no coming back from where she has been. Your best bet is to just kill her. Do not try to negotiate or demand that she cooperates. People underestimate her capabilities because of her size. Fooled me too! I didn't think she could shoot me. That is pretty much what happened. I'm guessing you'll need my written testimony or are you lame fucks recording this meeting? It's inadmissible because you did not offer me counsel. I want immunity before I say another word or testify to anything. No immunity equals no deal. Take me back to my cell until you have something to offer me".

Montez had grown a new pair of balls, despite what he had been through at Orakee. The guards came to escort him back to his tier, where he would meet his new bunk mate

CHAPTER 7

A.K.A. THE BEAR

Montez walked the halls with total confidence. He held his head up high as he walked past the other inmates. He wondered whose cell he was being escorted to because he bunked down the hall from where he was. He walked into his new cell and stopped once he seen a muscular man with his back turned towards the sink. That man would finish cutting a piss and turn towards Montez. He looked Tez up and down before sticking his unwashed hand out for a dap. Tez said; "Yo money, who are you, do I know you or something partna?"

The man replied, "I'm O.G. 9, also known as The Bear". Before O.G. could get another word of his introduction out, Montez had cut him off and said, "Oh yeah, I've heard talks of the infamous and legendary 9. Word is you offed nine people back when you were running the streets. You still have the people on the Kee shook. All they had do is mention your name and you could see the color leave their face out of fear. Wild man! You been down for about 20 years, huh O.G.?"

The Bear took over the conversation by saying, "You see that youngblood? You are already talking too much, and around here, that is a warning sign to me that you are a snitch. Whenever you hear shit, you keep it to yourself. You just volunteered information that I did not ask for."

No doubt that Montez was confused. He looked puzzled!

"As I was saying before you cut me off; You do not know me personally, but you know someone that is related to me. In fact, I am told that you knocked her up, played mind games with who you really were, and as a result, she is evading all authorities. She missed out on raising the twins and being there for the daughter she already had. We have plenty to rap about youngblood. I am Nicole's father. Word travels fast in here. I've heard all about the stuff that you have taken her through. I cannot say that I appreciate it. I put in a word to the warden at the Kee to have you transferred here because, once again; I hear shit and word around is that Devo spent top dollar to have you brutally raped and beaten. This was some form of payback for sleeping with her in the first place after you had been hired for protection.

Looks like you got too comfortable. They also said that when Devo was done emasculating you, he put you up for bid to everyone on the unit. Had I not pulled you out when I did, you would be filled with more dick than you can stand to count. That type of shit does not happen in here. I make sure that it doesn't. That is not what real men do. I'm not gon' rap you up, I am sure you are tired. We'll talk in the morning, imma show you the ropes around here."

The next morning came and The Bear had been showing Tez the ropes around Noakwood. Tez expressed how much different it was in comparison to Orakee. Most of the cats in Noakwood had been there over ten years or so. They just wanted to do their time with no infractions or time added; so, they could go home, those who was not there for the long haul. As time went on; The Bear would open up to Tez and take him under his wing. It was apparent that Montez had no father figure growing up. He was a survivalist and he had had a rough life. The Bear would get through to him as time went by.

One day as the pair was lifting weights, O.G. asked Tez if Nicole had ever told him about how her parents met. Tez said, "She spoke about it briefly, but always shut down because she was embarrassed that both of her parents were locked up and that she had been born through that bloodline". O.G. slammed the dumbbells down and paced the yard in anger.

He walked back towards Tez and said, "Nicole was eighteen when I got locked up. She thinks I walked out on her, but the truth of the matter is that I did not want her to see what I had become. I couldn't face her knowing I had let her down. She had heard some of the stories but not the ones that reveals just how monstrous I had gotten. LuAnn did a good job covering that up. I met Nicole's mother back in 1976. Her name is Latanya, but I called her FrootLoop. She was very vibrant and full of charisma. I could not help but notice she was a little loopy in the head. We had been on some Bonnie and Clyde shit. I sold drugs and she used that money to open two legitimate nightclubs. One for herself and one for LuAnn.

We ruled the streets back then. The bigger our operation got, the more manpower we needed. I always did my own dirty work. Mostly those who posed as a threat to my operation. If I wanted you dead then I had to be the one to do it. The man that passes the sentence, should deliver the punishment. I am down for life after being convicted of ten counts of murder in the first and second degree. I will not speak on it any further because I am in the appeals process after new evidence suggests that the witnesses colluded with the police to get a conviction. They just wanted me off the streets. I had gotten too powerful. The same officers on my payroll were the very ones to help take me down. They are dead now and dead men cannot talk. FrootLoop was right there beside me! Queen of the Castle. I practically raised Nicole by myself because her mother had killed 2 undercover detectives attempting to infiltrate her operation back in 1991. No doubt that woman earned that name. It could have gone different way but Loop despised snitches and police. She did not care that witnesses were around or that the detectives had bugs on them. I did my best with the help of Luann to raise Nicole. I could not give up the streets, had I just walked away years ago I wouldn't be here today".

The Bear poured out his heart and before he knew it; the guards had banged their batons on the fence ordering them to leave the yard. O.G. had gotten tired of talking so on the way back to their cell, he asked Tez if his father had been in his life. That is a conversation that he did not want to have. He was not ready to face those emotions and feelings of abandonment. Tez explain that he did not know his father. He had been killed while his mother was pregnant with him. Tez said, "all I know is that the bamma tried to rob a dude at the gas station and that dude left his ass".

The Bear's heart dropped because he knew that it was him that killed Montez's father. The universe is tricky like that. Montez's words ate at O.G. for six months before he would confess to Tez. He was trying to remove the burden and guilt he had carried all these years. O.G. also wanted to bring closure to Montez's family. Hurt people hurt people. He understood the pain that Tez had caused Nicole. O.G. was never convicted of that murder because it was a clear case of self-defense. Montez was not mad, however he was hurt and felt that the only reason 9 had taken him under his wing was because he knew what he had done. Tez also knew that O.G. did not go out looking to kill Montez Sr.

With one less burden to carry, O.G. continued to help Montez better himself. He had taken on the role of Tez's father. The uncomfortable conversation came up as to how they could help save Nicole from her own demise. Baby Girl was on a warpath. She craved the blood of all her enemies and would stop at nothing to get it. Tez confessed to O.G. that he had already told the detectives that Nicole murdered Nakyta and Al and is attempting to kill the judge and district attorney assigned to their cases. Bear laughed and said, "Damn if that ain't FrootLoop Jr". Montez said that he did not write a statement and that it was just a story he fabricated to get him transferred out of the Kee. There were no hard feelings between the two and as they went on to devise a plan to help Nicole get to the judge and DA, the warden of Noakwood stormed in their cell.

Warden Paul was close friends with O.G. and he had told him that Nicole went off the deep end and could not be stopped. She had killed Judge Conyers and her husband. She waited until the pair got home and shot them to death before they could get out their vehicle. Warden Paul threw his cell phone at O.G. and instructed him to stop Nicole. Even though The Bear had not talked to Nicole in years, he still knew how to contact her. He placed a call to her cell and surprisingly she answered. "BabyGirl, it's dad! What are you doing? Stop what you are doing and lay low. It is hot on you right now. This is a courtesy call. Sit tight until you hear from me again." Nicole said, 'Daddy? FUCK

YOU! And hung up the phone. The trio looked at each other in awe. They knew it would not end well. Warden Paul left and The Bear and Tez went on devising a plan to save Nicole. Reformed or not, Nicole is The Bear's BabyGirl, his heart! And everyone knows,

"You can't live without your heart"!!!

Find out what happens next in... Volume III – Wrath of Nicole

www.ingramcontent.com/pod-product-compliance
Lightning Source LLC
Chambersburg PA
CBHW031854170626
46807CB00004B/1730